THE SUPERHERO WITHIN

Super Drat

ADAM MAITLAND

iUniverse

THE SUPERHERO WITHIN
SUPER DRAT

iUniverse books may be ordered through booksellers or by contacting:

iUniverse
1663 Liberty Drive
Bloomington, IN 47403
www.iuniverse.com
1-800-Authors (1-800-288-4677)

ISBN: 978-1-5320-7570-4 (sc)
ISBN: 978-1-5320-7571-1 (hc)
ISBN: 978-1-5320-7572-8 (e)

Library of Congress Control Number: 2019910077

Print information available on the last page.

iUniverse rev. date: 07/22/2019

Chapter 1

I'M DEXTER, AND I'M DIFFERENT

My name is Dexter, but sometimes I don't like that name. I don't feel like it always fits who I truly am. I have tried other names, like Max and Zack. Once I even tried the name Bob, but I always seem to end up with the same name, Dexter. I guess sometimes I just want to be somebody else for a change.

When I was younger, I could never figure out what my brain wanted, which always made me confused and frustrated. My body would do things without me telling it to, and that just drove me crazy. My family tried to help. In fact, everybody tried to help me, like my teachers and strange adults my parents brought me to see. The strangers would have me sit on a couch or play silly games with them, but sometimes I felt more like I was under attack for something I could not control. Sometimes I could just be sitting, calmly playing with my favorite dragon toys, and then I would throw one of my dragons across the room, or I would try to put them in my mouth, or my legs would just start kicking the floor really fast and hard. A lot of the time, I would just start rubbing my hands together quickly. It was neat to feel the friction warm my hands, but other than that, I didn't know why I did it besides it giving me something to do with my hands when I felt uncomfortable.

It wasn't like I thought being different was the greatest thing in the world, but it wasn't my choice. In fact, I thought it was a curse at first. I also thought I must have done something wrong to be like this, but I couldn't think of anything I could have possibly done. It just seemed so unfair that the world I had to live in felt so distant and strange. I just couldn't figure out what people wanted from me. I did my best to control my body, especially in school, where we had to sit at our desks and pay attention to a lesson. Sometimes my brain just blurted out random words or sounds, like a dragon roaring, which upset the teacher because I was interrupting her lesson. Then, of course, I wanted to take my dragon toys out of my pocket and start playing with them, but no teacher wants you to play with toys when you are supposed to be listening and learning. When my legs started kicking, I usually hit a desk or chair, but sometimes I missed and kicked another student. I didn't mean to, but I couldn't control it. Then everyone got upset because it was hard for anyone to focus when a desk, chair, or student was being kicked.

I would have gladly paid more attention to people if I'd understood what they were saying. I would have done my homework if it made sense, and I would have even acted normal if my body would have just listened to me when I told it to. My frustration just kept building! I was finding it awfully difficult to be happy. Why did I have to be so different? Why couldn't I control my body, when I just wanted to be calm or when I was in class, trying to learn? This didn't happen all the time. Some days were pretty good, but when it did happen—in class, at recess, at home watching TV, or getting ready for bed—my body didn't do what it needed to, and then I had a hard time trying to figure out what to do. When I couldn't figure it out, I started crying or screaming. Simple things became more difficult, like sitting quietly in class, playing with other kids at recess, putting my dragon toys away, or putting on my pajamas, because I couldn't always get my body and brain to work together and just do what they needed to do.

I knew everyone cared about me, but sometimes I felt more alone when everyone was trying to fix me. I didn't understand how I was broken or what had happened to me that broke me. Everyone wanted me to act a certain way. "Sit quietly," they said. "Keep your body calm." They wanted me to try different things, and I truly felt bad when I wasn't. Sometimes I chose to do things that got people even more upset with me, like screaming at them to leave me alone, hitting or pushing desks and chairs, or running and trying to find a place to hide. I sort of understood that everyone just wanted me to be able to sit in class like everyone else, without kicking or blurting out sounds. They wanted me to be able to play with other kids at recess without getting frustrated that I couldn't play with my dragon toys. I absolutely loved my dragon toys and tried to bring them with me everywhere I went.

Apparently, you shouldn't bring your favorite dragon toys everywhere you go, because you should want to try new things, like playing tag with other kids or playing with different toys that other kids are playing with.

I felt like I couldn't win. I wanted to make everyone happy, but I certainly liked to do what I liked to do and felt like there was only so much I could do to control my body. I was starting to feel like I couldn't make anyone happy. I felt like people were always mad at me because I couldn't keep my body calm or wouldn't try new things.

I knew I had to figure out some way to fix myself and make everyone happy. There had to be a way to make everything better. I just needed to work harder to fit into this crazy world. I needed to solve this puzzle that was me in order to make sense of all the things my brain and body did.

My parents, teachers, and even some of my classmates tried to help me, and with their help, I soon began to learn something important about myself. I was different for a reason, but the longer it took to figure out why, the more frustrated I became.

It was so tough living in a world where I felt like an alien. People thought I did odd things, but they just made me me. I could sense that they thought I was different and didn't fit in with them. I used to believe that too. I figured if the kids around me thought I didn't belong, then I probably didn't. So, I never tried to be friends with them. I just kept to myself and created my own world inside my head. That was one reason I loved my dragon toys so much. They never thought I was different or got upset with me when I didn't do everything a certain way.

So, I created a world that worked the way I thought it should. I wasn't forced to do things or eat weird foods. In fact, I was able to fly with dragons. I loved dragons, all kinds of dragons—dragons that fly through the skies, swim through the seas, and make their homes in the mountains. They ruled the world I created.

I was accepted in my world, and it frustrated me so much when people tried to force me out of my world and into the real world. Why would I want to be in a world where I didn't fit in, when I could be in a world that I loved?

People kept pushing me out of my world though, which kept reminding me that something was still wrong with me. I couldn't figure out what it was that I did to be such a misfit. People are fascinating and curious creatures! As much as I loved to observe them, I knew in the back of my mind that I had to help them see beyond my differences.

By helping them, maybe then I wouldn't feel so out of place. Maybe then everyone, not just my dragons, would accept me. I wanted people to accept me for who I was, but I didn't know how to make that happen, until something amazing happened to me.

Chapter 2

IT'S TIME TO FIND OUT WHO YOU REALLY ARE

I soon discovered something exceptional about myself and realized that my differences made me quite special indeed.

All the things that make me seem strange and different are all key pieces to who I am as a person. Having supersharp senses, not knowing all the right words I want to say to people and feeling odd around other people—they are the pieces to the puzzle that make me the superhero I am today! That's right! I'm a superhero too, just like you!

Wait! You didn't know you are a superhero? Oh man! Maybe you forgot, maybe one of your archnemeses got ahold of your brain and made you forget about your superpowers, or maybe you just weren't aware of how powerful and gifted you truly are. It took me a while to figure it out, but luckily for you, I'm here to help!

Maybe if I tell you about some of my powers and how I use them, it will help you identify your own. Then we can work together and help each other become stronger. It's also nice to have some help when going on adventures, even if you are a superhero. Sometimes I can use help when choosing which power is best on a mission. You can use our time together as training for using your powers and becoming stronger. Putting in the effort to get better is everything when you're a superhero. Nobody's perfect, and as a superhero, I have made it my own personal mission to make sure people know that being different is perfectly normal.

Let me tell you a little bit about my powers. Here's the thing: what makes me different is, in fact, part of what makes me a superhero. My supersensitive hearing allows me to hear another person whispering from the other side of the room or hear cries for help from those who are in trouble. Being sensitive to everything I touch makes my whole body shiver. It doesn't matter how hot, cold, smooth or rough it is. This is how I absorb information about what I am touching. My supersmelling can often be one of my worst powers because some smells are just awful. It does, however, make it easier for me to find people and things that are missing, especially if I know their scent. It can get in the way of my eating, as some foods have really strong smells, which makes it difficult for me to want to eat them, unless it's chocolate chip cookies, of course. Even my hard time listening to people and talking with them is part of what makes me a superhero because I communicate differently with thoughts and pictures. This is especially handy when I am helping others that speak different languages. But like every superhero, there is always a main power that makes you unique compared to all the rest.

I've already mentioned that I love dragons and all for a good reason. My main superpower is the ability to call upon dragons whenever I need their assistance or their powers to use as my own. My interests in them began when I started seeing them in books and movies. Then I started reading and studying about them so I could understand all the different kinds of dragons. Now I can choose between all the different dragons to help me be the best superhero ever!

Learning I had superpowers wasn't easy. In fact, I was confused when I discovered this part of me. I thought about the world of dragons I had created. For some reason, I began thinking about a family of dragons. I don't know why I was thinking about a family of dragons, because usually I only thought about one dragon at a time. I wondered what its scales were like, what magical breath it had, and all the other unique qualities of each dragon.

Then, out of nowhere, the family of dragons I was thinking about appeared right in my bedroom. The mom and dad dragons were a little taller than me. They had beautiful white scales and wings that reflected the light and looked more like rainbows resting on their backs. Their two baby dragons had shiny scales, but the bigger one had bright-yellow scales and orange wings. The smaller one had grayish scales and black wings. I learned that the dad dragon was named Slyph and the mom was named Lumi.

Slyph would tell me all the time, "Dexter, it is essential for you to always stand up for yourself and use your voice the best you can to communicate with others. It is imperative to communicate so you can share and learn more about the world around you."

Lumi would share her wisdom with me by saying, "It is key to be aware of how you feel and learn how to take care of yourself when you might feel sad or mad. It is better to deal with a problem than to find ways to ignore it."

They all helped me to grow and learn about who I truly am. Once I learned about my superpowers, the family of dragons helped me to see my destiny as a superhero. They taught me that being a superhero meant I needed to be determined, responsible, assertive, and thoughtful.

I had no idea how I was going to remember all of that and save the world. I definitely doubted my abilities. What was I going to do with my new superpowers and hero's code?

Sol, the orange-scaled dragon, and Yue, the dark-gray dragon, both became my best friends. We played games together, read stories, and trained to use my superpowers and their dragon breath. We talked about times when we got upset, like if my schedule at school changed or when my dad picked me up late from school.

Sol explained to me, "Even when things don't go the way we want them to, we must be determined to do what is right, be responsible for our actions, be assertive when standing up for ourselves and our friends and be thoughtful toward how others are doing."

Yue told me, "Never forget the superhero you are. From this day on, your superhero identity will help you to constantly remember the hero's code and how great of a superhero you will be. You will forever be known as Super Drat!"

Since that day, I have worked hard to take my responsibilities of being a superhero seriously. Each of the letters in my superhero name Drat stands for a part of my hero's code: *D* for *determined*, *R* for *responsible*, *A* for *assertive*, and *T* for *thoughtful*. It helps me to remember to be determined to never give up and protect the special friends I make throughout my adventures. I work hard to be responsible for each decision I make, especially when I am helping others. I work to be assertive in helping people see that being different is not bad but what makes us all special in our own way. I stay thoughtful in order to show respect to all of those I protect.

I knew it was my destiny to protect the world and since then, I haven't stopped. Now, it's your turn to learn how you can help. You can be a superhero, just like you were always meant to be.

Chapter

3

LOOKS LIKE WE GOT TROUBLE!

O h no! My dragon senses are warning me about something. What are my dragon senses? Well, you know how I told you I have supersensitive hearing? It turns out that my sensitive hearing gives me the ability to hear calls for help. That's how I find out about my missions. Looks like we are heading out on our first mission together!

Why do I say "we"? You're coming with me. You know all about my secret identity now. It only makes sense that we team up and take down the bad guys together. Trust me— you're going to love this superhero stuff.

What about your powers? You still aren't sure what they are? Yeah, you're right. That might be a problem. Think about it. You might notice your superpower if you're able to run quickly from point A to point B. Maybe you zone out and end up somewhere else or in another time. You might notice the weather outside reflects how you are feeling or that you are exceptionally good at noticing specific details about a person or a place. You might even notice that you can read how people feel or what they think. Your powers might already be in place, but you just aren't aware of them yet. Don't worry, I'll keep you safe. And who knows? Maybe going on your first mission will help you find out what your superhero powers are. Come on, let's go! I am sure everything will be just fine. The only way to find out what kind of superhero you are is to try out using different powers you think you might have and see what happens next.

It looks like this mission is going to be taking us to the Island of Great Inventions. What a mission for your first time! You've never heard of that place? Don't worry. Part of being special, like me, is that your mind is open to seeing what other people can't see. I think you will understand more as we work together, but just remember for now that being special allows you to see some of the most amazing things, like dragons, islands of mythical creatures, and other incredible superheroes. It is truly a gift.

It looks like we are going to be facing Creepo the Minotaur. According to my records, he is superstrong and supertall and can be supermean. He is ruining a village on the island, and the villagers don't know what to do. I'm glad you are coming with me on this mission. We are going to need to work together to make this mission successful.

We are going to need a ride to this place, and I can assure you that a taxi or a bus won't get us to where we are going.

I'd better start calling Tenshi. What am I doing with my hands? Flapping my hands and fingers like this creates a signal that helps me call to the dragons. My various hand movements call a particular dragon. When the dragons flap their wings, they can fly, but they can also send signals to their friends. It's kind of like when you use a phone, you have to dial a certain number to call a certain person.

Then, as I make the right pattern with my hands and fingers, I start to glow. When I glow, a doorway opens for the dragons to come right to me.

Ah! Perfect! Here he is. This is Tenshi. Look how big he is. He doesn't even fit inside my house because of his huge brown- and black-striped wings. I love his golden-brown scales and his bright golden eyes. He has large smooth spikes that go down his back and make it easier to sit on him and to have something to hold on to when I am flying on his back. He might look upset, but don't mind him. He loves flying me all over the place. He was one of the first dragons I called upon after I met that family of dragons. Now he is one of my best friends. I know I can always turn to him when I get frustrated. He doesn't always say a lot, but it helps to know that he is there just to listen if I need him.

So, come on! Let's get going before it's too late. Have no fear. Tenshi is the fastest dragon around. He tends to be quite modest. He doesn't like it when I tell everybody how great he is, but I just can't help myself.

Chapter

4

SOME THINGS YOU SHOULD KNOW

old on tight. Here we go!
Tenshi says you're as light as a feather, which is great because that means he can fly even faster. He says we will be at the island soon.

How do I know what Tenshi is saying? It is part of my superpowers. It can be challenging for me to listen to people, even more so when I am trying to talk to people. It's hard for me to listen because when I hear a lot of the words out loud, they get jumbled up in my brain and I don't always hear the words in the correct order. I also struggle because I like talking more, especially about all the dragons. But sometimes people get bored with what I have to say, which is kind of sad because I think that what I have to say is pretty interesting. Did you know that just about every culture in the world has some type of dragon either in their symbols or in their stories?

People may think I am rude because I'm shy, but I am only shy because I am not comfortable around other people. Sometimes people even get angry or upset with me because it seems like I'm not listening to them, but I am just trying to read their thoughts and hoping they can read mine.

My superpower allows Tenshi to send his thoughts right to my brain, so they don't get jumbled up. I am able to perfectly understand what he is thinking, and he knows exactly what I am thinking. It turns out that my hard time listening and talking to people is due to the fact that I communicate better by thought, just like the dragons. When I call upon the dragons, they talk to me using their thoughts and ideas. They tell me how they feel by showing me colors in my head that match their feelings. If the dragon is mad, I see red in my mind, or if the dragon is sad, I see blue.

That is why I have a hard time showing how I feel. It's all in my head. The dragons let me know what they want me to know in my head, and I am able to do the same to them, but most people don't always see what I am showing them in their heads. It gets frustrating, and people are easily confused, especially when I try to read their thoughts and all they do is keep talking and talking. I end up lost and confused and even more frustrated. It can certainly get difficult at times.

I try to understand the words people are saying, but I respond to them with my thoughts. However, they don't understand this way of communicating.

Like every superhero, I work hard to learn the language of the people I must protect, and I try every day to get a little better at talking like them. Remember that being thoughtful of others shows respect and gets others to respect you as well.

Okay, so there are a few things you need to know about being a superhero. First of all, you must have a secret identity. Luckily for me, I'm a student in school, and I wear glasses when I'm not out fighting crime. Glasses can hide anyone's identity if they wear the right pair and keep their hair a certain way. It sounds funny, and it is kind of funny, but it's true and it works. Masks also work, but I don't like things covering my entire face.

When I have to be a superhero, I'm known as Super Drat, but when I'm not out saving the world, then I am Dexter, the kid who goes to school and tries to fit in the best he can. Honestly, between you and me, a lot of the time it is harder being Dexter than it is being Super Drat.

Having a secret identity keeps the people I know safe and out of danger. Otherwise, my enemies will try to use my family and friends as hostages to trick me into doing bad things. It happened to me once, and that is why the dragons made me a special superhero costume. It hasn't happened again. When I first started out as a superhero, I did not want to wear a mask at all. My dragons told me I should, but masks can be so uncomfortable. I learned my lesson though.

I had to go off on a mission. I had to rescue a family of gryphons that were being attacked by a hunter who wanted their talons. I was able to save the family, but because I didn't wear a mask, the hunter found where I lived. I had to save my family. It was pretty scary, but the gryphons and my dragons helped me stop the hunter and showed him how he could use his skills to help the gryphons. In return, the gryphons would help.

The hunter wanted their talons to make superstrong daggers to help protect his family. Well, gryphons love to get their talons sharpened and cleaned. As long as the hunter promised to protect his family and the gryphons, the gryphons promised to share their talon clippings to help him make stronger daggers. It was pretty interesting how everything worked out in the end because it just took everyone sitting down and figuring out what the real problem was. Although my family was safe, and everything else worked out, I didn't want my family to have to be in the middle of one of my missions again.

So, I am counting on you to not tell anybody my secret identity, and you can trust in me to not tell anybody about yours.

The costume is the next crucial piece of being a superhero. Your costume represents who you are as a superhero. It also protects you when fighting the bad guys. You don't want to wear too many things, and you definitely want to make sure all the tags are cut off before wearing it. Those tags drive me nuts.

You also don't want to wear things that are too hot or too light. Luckily for me, I grew up loving the cold. This drove most people crazy because I would be fine going outside on a cold winter day in my swimsuit and nothing else. You got it, another superpower. I am immune to different temperatures, especially, cold temperatures. I don't like getting too hot, but I had no problem dealing with the cold. That is why my costume is nice and light but still covers most of me for a vital reason.

You know how I told you I'm sensitive to touch? Well, it's because with everything I touch, I absorb information from it. If something feels peculiar, then it can make my brain go superfast because of all the information I'm absorbing. Once I touch something, my brain starts taking in information about how it feels, whether it's warm, cold, smooth, or rough. Then I start trying to figure out what I can do with whatever I am touching, whether it can be used to play a game or as a weapon, or if it will hurt me or keep me safe. My brain tries to tell me everything about the object I am touching, like what it might do or not do and how I might make it better or use it to build something new. This can set me into a weird mood. That is why my costume is designed to cover my hands and feet, so I can control what I touch.

My helmet doesn't cover my entire face, because it just feels too odd to be fighting the bad guys and having my face completely covered. Plus, I can see more when I'm not wearing a mask. I wear a helmet to protect my head when flying on Tenshi and also in battle. It also protects my ears from superloud sounds that can make me go crazy. It is tough having supersenses, but I've learned to work with them. I also have to be careful not to break my glasses, so my helmet has built in lens to protect my eyes, help me see better, and block bright lights.

Then there is the cape. It's optional, but come on, a cape is just so cool. Plus, all the greatest superheroes have one. The cape makes you look wiser and stronger, and it can protect you from almost anything, especially when you want to hide from bright lights or people who aren't nice. Just make sure it's not so long that you're always stepping on it or falling over. That's embarrassing. Since I don't like wearing things tight around my neck, I wear my cape like a jacket. It is made out of dark red dragon hairs, which are lightweight, but extremely strong. It protects me from any weather changes, especially when flying. It also acts like a shield against different attacks like punches, lightning, and fire. In fact, it protects me from practically everything.

Finally, the main part of being a superhero is having a code. Luckily for me, that dragon family gave me my own hero's code. Before every mission, I always remind myself to be determined (never give up, even when something seems impossible), be responsible (do what you are expected to do, and accept the results), be assertive (stand up for what you believe in, and be yourself), and be thoughtful (respect and think of others). It's also lucky for me that the first letters of these words spell out my superhero name (which I love, by the way), so I can never forget it. You can use my hero's code for now until you find or make your own.

I think you are ready to start your superhero training. Tenshi agrees. He thinks you have a lot of potential, and he doesn't say that to just anybody.

Super DRAT

Determined
Responsible
Assertive
Thoughtful

Chapter

5

TIME TO MAKE A PLAN

t looks like we finally made it here. It's time to be a superhero. Do you want to give Tenshi his crystal treats in exchange for the ride he gave us? They are crystals you can find in the earth. They come in all different shapes and sizes. Tenshi loves the ones that are round and dark blue. Don't worry, he won't bite. Dragons don't eat humans. That's just a silly myth to scare people. Dragons actually eat crystals. It's all right. Give him his treat, and we can start heading over to the village.

The village looks like a bunch of palm trees. The roofs are made to look like palm tree leaves, and the outside of the huts look like the trunk of the tree. This is how the village is able to blend in and stay hidden from outside visitors. It is a pretty sneaky defense system, if you ask me.

When I heard the call for help, I knew we would be heading to this island. I heard the village was being attacked by Creepo. He is incredibly strong, and I heard he was destroying everything he saw with his long, pointy horns; strong, large arms; and hooved feet.

Oh no! Do you see all the smoke over there? That is not a good sign. Apparently, Creepo already showed off his superstrength. This isn't good. We'd better have a look around. It looks to me like Creepo is already gone, so now we will have a chance to investigate.

Look at all the damage. All these homes have been torn apart and stomped to pieces. Man, I can't wait to get my hands on Creepo and make him pay for doing all of this. Seeing others being mean gets me so frustrated. I just want to scream. This just isn't fair!

One … two … three … breathe. Okay. I'm all right. Sometimes I need to remember to take a deep breath and stay focused. If I don't, then my senses can go into overload, I can get extremely upset, and I forget all about the mission. I might start screaming and shouting, and then it becomes even harder for me to calm down.

Look! Over there, something is moving. Let's go see who or what it is.

It's one of the villagers. You might think he looks peculiar, but it is probably your first time seeing a goblin. Goblins might look small and odd, but they are exceptionally intelligent and put a lot of effort into creating some of the most advanced gadgets ever. They have their own special ability to create new inventions out of just about anything they can get their hands on. Their huts look like normal palm trees, but everything inside is set up for the goblins' workshops and living spaces. The goblins might be small, but they need a lot of space for everything they are working on. The multiple levels of their huts are built up the look-alike trunk of the palm tree so they can have a workshops on each level for each of the different projects they are working on. Then they put their bedroom at the very top. This way they can keep an eye out for uninvited guests. They like to have multiple workshops because they tend to work on several projects at the same time but want to make sure all their materials stay organized.

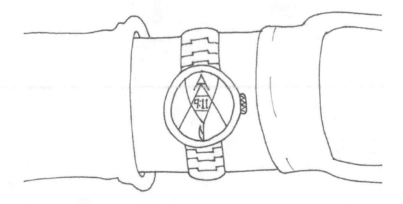

See this watch? A goblin friend of mine gave it to me a while back when I saved him from almost drowning at a pool party. He wasn't a good swimmer, but he wanted to be cool like his friends and jumped off the diving board. Luckily for him, I was there to save him from drowning and later on teach him how to swim. So, in return, he made me this super high-tech watch.

You want to know what it does? It changes me from Dexter to Super Drat in seconds. It's incredible, isn't it? All I have to do is press this button, and it will instantly change me into or out of my costume. It will also repair my costume if it gets damaged. Plus, the watch digitally tells time, so I can read it, and it is water-resistant, so I can swim with it.

Okay, stay focused. Back to the problem at hand. Let's get this guy out of here. Maybe, once we wake him up, we can figure out why Creepo is doing this. You can see from all this damage just how strong Creepo can be, but if we work together, I am sure we will be fine. I know one thing is for sure! We need to stop Creepo and save the goblins and what's left of their village. Look how many of their huts he has already destroyed. All the broken windows, computers, ripped-up plans, and gear have been thrown all over the place. We can't allow any more destruction to happen.

Here, give me a hand, please. You get his legs, and I'll get his arms. We can carry him over to those palm trees. Goblins might look small, but they weigh a ton. Get a good grip. Okay, here we go. On three. One ... two ... three ... ugh! It feels like he weighs more than a ton. Let's move quickly but carefully. We don't want to drop him.

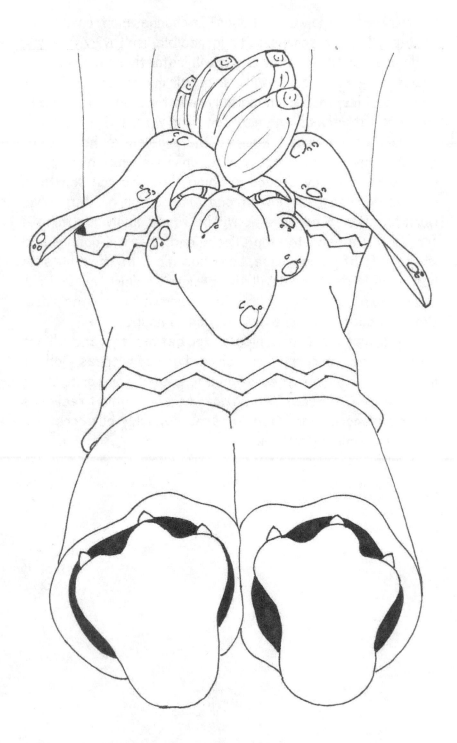

6

TIME TO MAKE A CHOICE

I t's a good thing we have Tenshi to help us. When he is around, he helps me to translate what other people or creatures are saying. He is able to take their words and mine and use colors and pictures to help all of us understand one another.

Mr. Goblin doesn't look like he is hurt too badly. Look, he is opening his eyes. I better check and see how he's feeling.

"How are you feeling, Mr. Goblin?"

"The name's Fred, and man! My head is really hurting. Thanks for getting me out of there. I hope my friends are all right too. What a surprise attack that was. We didn't know what hit us until it was too late. I can't believe Creepo would do this!"

"I am sure your friends will be fine, Fred, but you have to tell us what is going on. Do you know why Creepo is doing this to your village?"

"Because Creepo is a jerk! He is a bully, and no one likes him! Just comes stomping into our village, acting like everything is his, and thinking he can tell us what to do. We can't help that we are smarter than he is. He thinks he can push us around because we're smaller than he is. He is just a big stupid minotaur, picking on us for no reason!"

"Hmm … do you call him bad names like that to his face?"

"Only after he starts picking on us. Why shouldn't we? He comes into our workshops and breaks everything he touches, and now he destroyed our entire village! This isn't the first time either. We need to do something that will stop Creepo for good!"

Oh boy! Fred certainly is mad, and it sounds like the other goblins are too. I can't say that I blame them. I would get pretty mad too if people came into my room and broke all my toys. What do you think we should do?

If Creepo is as big of a bully as Fred says he is, then we need to stop him. Just because he is mad doesn't mean he gets to pick on the goblins. There are better ways to deal with anger. We have to help the goblins. I have two dragons in mind that I think could help us out on this mission, but I need your help deciding which one I should call.

The first dragon I am thinking about is Brutus. He is a big dragon—I mean huge! He is truly friendly but trust me—you don't want to get on his bad side. His large body is covered in white and sky-blue scales. He has two enormous white wings that rest upon his back when he isn't flying around in the sky. If the spikes all over his body aren't intimidating enough, he also has lightning breath. Then there is his superstrength. His large muscled arms are so strong that he plays catch using a comet from the sky. If he has to fight, he will, especially if it's to protect his friends, but usually with one look at him, his enemy runs off scared. Brutus won't run after his enemy, but if his enemy decides to attack and he has to fight, he will—and most likely will win.

I'm not sure if he is the best choice. Should we fight Creepo with our strength? Let me tell you my other idea, and then we can decide.

The other dragon is supersmart. Intal is the dragon that loves to learn and think. She knows something about everything. Some of the dragons say she can help you think things out even when you are completely frustrated. She is not much of a fighter, but she can come up with these incredible plans to take on any problem she faces and solve it without anyone getting hurt. She is a lot smaller than Brutus and doesn't have the large muscles. Her dark-purple scales cover her sleek and long body. She has the prettiest white-and-purple-feathered wings that are supersoft and comfortable to lie back on when she is reading her favorite books. She sounds like a good choice to me, but I don't know if she is the best choice to take on Creepo. Should we fight Creepo with our smarts?

Look over there! It's Creepo! He's back! Oh wow, he is three times bigger than I am. We'd better make a choice quick. Oh no, he just destroyed something else!

"Yeah, he did. That bully just destroyed our library. I hope the books are okay. As much as we goblins like to build and create things, we also love to read. That makes me so angry, seeing all the books being smashed!"

"Don't worry, Fred. We are going to take care of this once and for all!"

Okay, partner, it's up to you. Tell me what dragon to call forth quickly so we can stop Creepo from destroying anything else. Should we call upon Brutus or Intal?

If you think I should call upon Brutus, turn to Chapter 7. If you think I should call upon Intal, turn to Chapter 8.

Chapter

7

BRUTUS

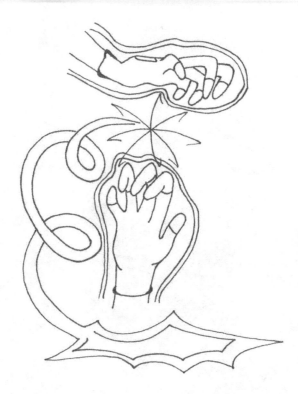

Okay, so you're thinking that Brutus would be a good choice. Then let's put it to the test. I hope this works because we have to stand up for these goblins and protect their homes. I'd better call Brutus. You might want to stand back. Like I said, Brutus is huge. There you go, a little bit farther. Keep going. Um, okay, right there.

Here he is.

"Hi, Brutus. How's it going? You are looking quite robust today. I love how your scales let you blend into the sky. Whoa! Brutus, watch that lightning breath."

He does that when he is in a great mood. He loves to show off.

"Okay, Brutus, here's the problem. Creepo over there has been bullying our friend Fred and the other goblins that live here in this village. He has been destroying their village, and we just watched him stomp on their library. The goblins are tired of this and want him to go away. Do you think you can help us out, Brutus?"

"Super Drat, you know how I feel about bullies. Nobody should be picked on, especially when they are as tiny as these goblins. I can almost fit three of them in my hand. Creepo might be upset about something, but that doesn't give him the right to pick on this village. Let's find Creepo and make sure he knows he can't act this way toward our friends."

"Awesome, Brutus! I greatly appreciate your help. Let's go take care of business."

Here's the plan. I'm going to call Creepo over to me, and Brutus is going to fly behind him. We will tell him to leave, and then Brutus will sneak up behind him and scare him away for good. We just have to watch out for Creepo's charge. You don't want to get hit by a charging minotaur—trust me. We'd better hurry! I think Creepo is about to destroy something else.

"Hey, Creepo! Yeah, you! I am Super Drat, and my friends and I want you to leave right now! The goblins don't want you here and they definitely don't want you destroying their things, so leave and never return. You have no reason to be mean to them, and we won't let you destroy any more of their village."

That seem to make him even more mad. He is staring right at us and kicking his hooves back and forth. I think he is going to charge at us. His eyes are getting red, his nostrils are getting bigger, and he's moving his hooves back and forth even faster. Remember, we can't back down. We have to be assertive and stand up for what we believe in. We won't let him hurt the goblins anymore. I better say something.

"Go away, Creepo! You are just being mean! You are being a big bully! We don't want to fight you, but you're not welcome here! Go away!"

Uh-oh! Brutus, quick, fly off into the sky and get ready. Creepo is stomping his large black hooves back into the ground which clearly means he wants to charge forward and fight us.

"I told you, Creepo, we aren't here to fight you. We will defend the goblins and their homes if we have to, but your best choice would be to just leave and never come back."

He actually looks like he is even more outraged. You can see the rage growing in his eyes, the hairs on the top of his head are sticking straight up, and his pointy brown ears are pulled back.

Listen! Do you hear that? His breathing is getting heavier.

Watch out! He is charging right at us, and he is coming in fast.

"Brutus! Now! Phew! Nice work, Brutus. Even though your giant stature can be hard to miss, you did a great job flying in from behind to catch Creepo off guard.

"Hey, Creepo, if you are wondering whose claws those are holding you up in the air, just look up. Nice job, Brutus! Just keep holding him until he stops fighting to get out of your grip."

Sometimes when I get really angry, I like to get squeezed. Kind of like a hug, but I just like to feel the pressure on my body. I might run to my mom or dad and they will squeeze me with their hands and arms until I can calm down. It looks like Creepo isn't trying to fight Brutus anymore. I think we can let Creepo go and hopefully he will leave.

"You can let him go, Brutus.

Creepo, you need to know there is always someone stronger. You might be big and strong but using your strength to hurt others and destroy things is never okay. You better not bother us anymore. Plus, you don't have any friends to help you out. The goblins, my friends, and I will always work together and help one another."

Oh boy, I don't think this is working out the way I hoped it would. It looks like he might charge again. Yup, his nostrils are getting bigger, he's breathing heavier, and he is moving his large, sharp hooves back and forth. He actually wants to fight, but we are ready for this. Here he comes! You might want to back up.

"Brutus! Lend me your strength!"

Watch this! Brutus is sharing his superstrength with me. When I start to glow, I will be as strong as Brutus is, and I will be able to stop Creepo and force him to go somewhere else, so he won't cause any more destruction to this village!

"Ah! Gotcha by your horns, Creepo! You might be big and strong, but I am stronger! How do you like being stopped by someone smaller than you? I might not be as gigantic as you are, but I have the strength of Brutus flowing through me.

Now like I said before, go away and leave my friends alone! Don't ever come back! Now, I am going to make you soar through the air like Brutus. Hope you don't mind going for a spin. One spin around, two spins around, three spins around, and off you go! *Hyah!*"

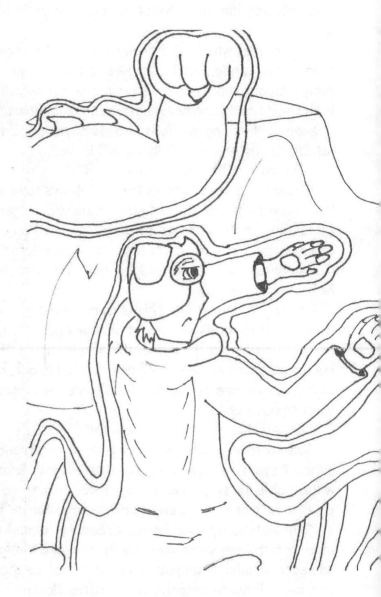

Don't worry, he won't get hurt. I threw him toward the sea. Once he swims back to shore, hopefully he will have cooled off and know that it will not be a good idea to come back. Fred and the other goblins should be safe.

"Thanks for your help, Brutus. We couldn't have done it without you. Once again, your strength is unlike anyone else's I know and love it when you share your strength with me."

Oh, I'm fine. Don't worry about me. Thanks to Brutus, I was able to use his strength to be stronger than Creepo. Plus, I don't feel pain as easily as other people. So, I won't even feel the things that might hurt some people. A lot of people get worried about me, but when I'm out saving the world, I'm not focused on my pain. Instead, I'm making sure that everyone is safe, even the bad guys, just like Creepo. I'm sure I didn't hurt him, but I'm also sure my point was made that he is no longer welcome in the goblins' village. I better make sure Fred is okay. I saw him run behind some rocks during the fight.

"Hey, Fred, you can come out now. Creepo is gone."

"Thank you so much, Super Drat, and your friends too. You guys sure did save the day. Look! There are all my friends. You were right! They're all okay! Once we get this place cleaned up, maybe you'll have time to celebrate this victory."

"Sure, that sounds great, and we can even help clean up. Come on! This shouldn't take long if we all work together."

I better let Brutus head back home. He could use a good rest after all he did to help us.

"Thanks again for your help, Brutus. You can go back home now. I think we can handle things from here. See you later."

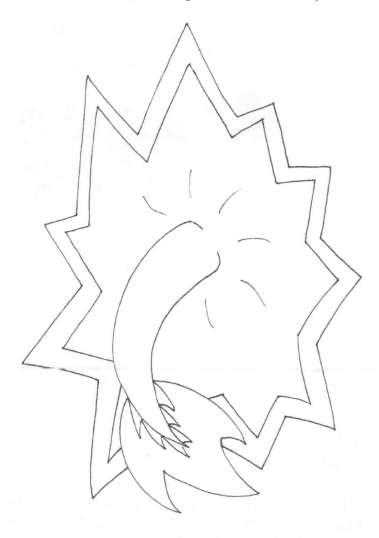

Wow! These goblins sure do know how to party. Look at all this great food. Pizza and macaroni and cheese, my favorites! Wow! Look at all the cookies. This victory celebration is wonderful. Look over there! The goblins are dancing.

Do you like to dance? It isn't one of my favorite things to do, but it can be fun when you are with friends. Look at the tiny, green goblins go. They just love hopping around and whipping around their long colorful hair. Did you know that when they are out trying their new gadgets, like their jet packs, if they think there might be danger around, they quickly let their colorful hair fall all around them, bury their feet, and wear their dark brown clothing so they look like plants? I always wondered why they wore those brown clothes, especially when they can make such amazing things, but it just makes it harder to find them.

Do they know how to dance, or what? Look at them spinning and flipping all over the place. This is fantastic! Even though it's kind of loud and there are a lot of goblins around, it's all right. Sometimes it is good to experience things you're not always comfortable with. I learned that it's just another way to become a better superhero.

I used to struggle being in large crowds, especially if I didn't know anyone. Recess at school was difficult for me. I would sometimes throw fits by screaming, crying, or hitting the floor just to avoid having to go to recess and being around the other students. Then, one day, my teacher introduced me to one student. His name was Max. Max was in my class. He was about the same height as me, but he had red hair and green eyes, whereas my hair is yellow, and I have gray eyes. I noticed that he had a book about dragons. It was one of my absolute favorite books. Max and I ended up talking about dragons during all of recess. We had so much fun we did it again for the next couple of days. Then Max asked me to go outside to recess with him and the other kids. Since Max was going to play outside with me, I decided to go without crying or screaming. We had even more fun playing on the swings, sliding down the slides, and running around, pretending to be dragons. Other kids joined us, and I started to get less nervous when other people were around me. I am not always comfortable in crowds now, but I can handle them a lot better and no longer just scream and hit the floor.

Do you hear something? It sounds like trees falling down and somebody stomping angrily into the ground. I wonder what it could be. It's getting louder. Did you feel that? The whole ground just rumbled. Something is wrong.

Oh no! Look over there. Something is coming out from the trees. Wait, I think I see something or someone. It is something that looks to be awfully big. I can hear it breathing loudly. Whoever it is is pushing the trees right over and seems to be moving fast. Do you smell that? It kind of smells like the sea.

I know who it is! I think we are about to have an even bigger problem on our hands. I guess Brutus might not have been the best choice to deal with Creepo.

Using my strength to make Creepo feel weaker must have only made him angrier. Sometimes trying to be tougher and fighting back when someone is upsetting you isn't the best way to solve your problem but have no fear.

The best part about making mistakes is that you can always learn from them and, as a superhero, become even more powerful for the next time you try. We are determined to help the goblins, but this time we will try something different. This time we will call Intal and see if she can help us. Here I go.

INTAL

"Hello, Intal. How are you doing today? Your dark purple scales look well polished, and your feathered wings seem extra fluffy. I always know you're in a good mood when your scales are so vivid. Unfortunately, I called to you because we have a problem and need your help. First, you should know that Creepo has been bullying the goblins and ruining their village. You probably already started thinking of a plan. Do you mind helping us out?"

"Your compliments always make me smile, Super Drat. I did take a few minutes away from reading one of my favorite books about plants using photosynthesis to create the food they need to survive and producing the oxygen we need to breathe. You know science is one of my favorite subjects."

"I know you love science, Intal, but we could use your help."

"Right, right, of course. My apologies. I love to share knowledge with anyone and everyone. Like I was saying, I understand the trouble you and your friends are dealing with and feel I could provide you with another way to go about this problem.

"I can see that Creepo is even more upset now than he was before, when he destroyed the village. Did you first try to talk with Creepo and find out why he was bullying the goblins? If you did, and he is just doing this to be mean, then I have a few ideas for what we could do next. We could set a trap to stop him and then wait until he is calm to let him go. We could get the goblins to create a mind-controlling device to make Creepo stop and do something else. Hmm ... let me think. What else could we do?"

"Whoa, Intal! I get it, I get it. You've got a lot of ideas, and I'm happy that you are willing to help us. This is great, but one plan at a time. We want to make sure we do this right. What do you mean, did we talk with Creepo about why he was bullying the goblins? The goblins don't care why. They just want him to leave them alone. The goblins are tired of him messing up their stuff. We just saw him smash their library, and I know how much you love books, Intal. So, you can understand why the goblins are so upset. Why would they invite him to join in their fun? He seems like he is just plain mean. Okay, okay, I will ask."

"Hey, Fred, Intal would like to know if you or any of the other goblins ever invited Creepo to join you during any of your activities?"

"We used to, but then he kept breaking all the things we created. He didn't even fit in our work spaces. We had to rebuild our homes so many times after he came to join in our activities, so we just stopped inviting him. I mean why would we want to invite him back?"

"Oh, I see. Wow, Intal, you always know the right questions to ask."

She thinks that even though Creepo is being mean, we still need to be thoughtful about how he might feel or what he might want. He may not be destroying everything because he is mean, but because he is trying to tell us something.

We have to be responsible and take care of this mission in a way that both the goblins and Creepo can be happy. It might sound impossible, but that is why we are superheroes. We take the impossible and make it work. We think outside the box. So, I guess the plan is to try to talk with Creepo and see what we can do to help him make better choices.

"Intal, will you come with us just in case we need your support?"

"Of course, Super Drat."

"Oh good, then this should hopefully go smoother than what we tried last time."

Okay, so now that I have you and Intal, let's see if we can get Creepo to talk with us. I will start by asking him with a calm voice.

"Excuse me, Creepo, do you think we could talk with you for a little bit? We wanted to see what is going on. If there is a problem, maybe we can help solve it together."

He looks even more outraged than before, and I don't blame him. He must be so frustrated. He probably can't even think clearly enough to talk with the goblins to solve his problem. I know when I get frustrated, I just want to scream, but luckily, I know I have my friends and family and the dragons there to help me.

"The responsible thing might not always be the easiest way, but if it's the right way, you have to try. When you do what's right, then the mission will more than likely be a success."

"You're right, Intal, and we can't be scared or cruel to Creepo just because he was mean. We have to treat him the way we would want to be treated."

I will try this again. I just have to remember to use a calm voice when I talk to Creepo.

"Hold on, Creepo, please! I am sorry for any misunderstandings and would like to take some time to listen to your side of the story and see if we can help you out. I know it can be hard to trust someone you don't know that well, but sometimes having someone new to listen to your problems can help you find a solution. Please, give us a chance to help."

It looks like he is getting ready to charge us, and we definitely don't want to get hit by those horns. We are going to have to defend ourselves.

"We shouldn't fight back, Super Drat."

"But, Intal, he will hurt us if we don't fight back. Then he will probably think he can bully us because he is stronger and bigger."

"We need to keep trying to calm him down. We can defend ourselves by watching his movements. He charges pretty fast, but once he is running, he can't turn very easily. We can use that knowledge to dodge his attack and move to a safer spot."

"Intal, I understand what you're saying, but look at how red his eyes are, and his nostrils are flaring from his heavy breathing. His hooves are moving even faster now. I don't know, Intal. I think this might be impossible."

"Super Drat, remember to be thoughtful and to keep your mind open to what is going on and how others are feeling. People used to think that just because you got frustrated, you were going to do something bad, but you were actually trying to calm yourself down. It was just difficult for you, but you were eventually able to calm yourself. Sometimes you even needed help from your parents, a friend, or even your favorite dragon toy. We have to help Creepo calm down. Keep trying to talk to him with a calm and friendly voice. Let him know you don't want to fight. Keep your body relaxed and your breathing calm and express your thoughts clearly so Creepo understands exactly what you are trying to tell him."

"Okay, Intal, I will do my best to be thoughtful and calm."

Let's see if we can help Creepo calm down and find out why he attacked the village. First, I am going to take a deep breath and count down. Five, four, three, two, one. I'm relaxing my body and taking another deep breath. Now let's talk to Creepo.

"Please listen to me, Creepo. We are not here to fight with you. We truly want to listen and hear what you have to say if you would just give us a chance."

Hmm ... I think maybe since we are standing right in front of Creepo, he probably thinks we are challenging him.

I have an idea, if you are willing to try. It always made me feel better when the person who was trying to calm me down was sitting down and we didn't have to look directly at each other. See those logs over there? We can all slowly move over there and have a seat. Let's see if Creepo will join us.

"What do you think, Creepo? Will you sit with us on the logs?"

"Fine, but you go sit down first, so I know it isn't a trap and you aren't just going to throw me into the sea again. That did *not* help me calm down at all!"

"Sure, of course we will go first. Okay, slowly now. Let's all have a seat."

I certainly hope this works.

"Okay, Creepo, whenever you are ready to join us, we just want to talk. No more fighting."

It looks like he is calming down. He isn't kicking his legs back and forth anymore, and it sounds like his breathing is slowing down a little bit.

Now remember we are not here to argue with Creepo or to tell him to get lost. We need to make sure we treat him with respect—you know, the same way we or the goblins want to be treated. If we get upset, we have to do our best to take deep breaths, calm ourselves, and focus on making this mission successful.

Chapter

9

THE SOLUTION

"**T**hanks for sitting down with us, Creepo. I'm sure we have a lot to talk about, but we want to hear what you have to say first. So, whenever you're ready to talk, just let us know. We'd like to understand why you've been bullying the goblins—"

"Bullying the goblins? They're the ones who were mean to me first. They make the coolest things, and I love watching them in their workshops when they invited me, but because I'm too big and broke a few things here and there, they never invited me back. Even when I begged them to let me see what they were working on, they just slammed the door in my face. I felt so left out. How would you feel Super Drat if they did that to you?"

"I agree with you, Creepo. That would be pretty frustrating. I definitely don't like to feel left out of anything that I find interesting. Fred, do you have anything to say."

"We only did that because Creepo is too big to be in our workshops. Every time we finished building something, he ended up breaking it. Creepo, you are just too big for our small village."

"I know, but it's not like I meant to break all your stuff. I was trying to be careful and move out of your way. I wanted to help, but I just didn't know how to. Super Drat, I didn't mean to break all their stuff. I know I'm big, but what can I do?"

"I think I might have a solution if you guys are willing to listen, but it's going to take both the goblins and you, Creepo, to be flexible and work together."

"Sure, Super Drat. What do you think we should do?"

"Well, Fred, I was thinking since so much of the village is ruined—"

"Sorry about that."

"It is always a good start to apologize, Creepo, especially when you know you were wrong for destroying this village just because you were angry. However, it might not be such a bad thing. Perhaps, you and the goblins could rebuild the village so that it's big enough for them to work and you to join them. Then they might be able to build even bigger projects for you to look at, play with, and even help with. You might even be inspired to start building your own projects."

"That's a great idea, Super Drat! Creepo, if you can help us rebuild the village, we could make workshops big enough for you to see and learn what we're doing. We have some projects we wanted to try but need someone who's strong and tall to help put it all together. Would you be interested in that?"

"Of course, Fred! You goblins build the most incredible things I have ever seen. All I actually wanted was to learn how you did it, and it hurt my feelings when I was told that all the goblins thought I was the stupidest thing alive and were planning on building something that would get rid of me forever! I got so angry. I just didn't know what to do."

"Someone told you *what*? Yes, we have called you some not-so-nice words, and we are truly sorry for that, but we would never build something to get rid of you forever. In fact, we wanted to create a book for you that would show you how to make some of the projects you liked the most, which we were working on until it got smashed in the library. We thought if we gave you the book, then you wouldn't need to be in our workshops. I can't believe someone would do something so horrible! Who would say something like?"

"Hmm. Fred, I think I might have an idea of who is behind this. It sounds like an old enemy of mine."

"Who, Super Drat? Who would be so cruel to tell me such a lie about what the goblins were planning?"

"The Rumors! They're a group of supervillains known for spreading gossip and lies using their own powers of deception. Seeing how angry you got, Creepo, you must have met Aggro. He is cruel. He can make you angry over the smallest things, and the angrier you get, the more powerful he becomes. He is only one of the many Rumors that I have been up against."

"The Rumors once made everyone think I was a supervillain and not a superhero. People had a hard time trusting me because the Rumors kept making me look bad, until I was finally able to prove they were the villains and nothing more than a bunch of liars. Perhaps they're planning something even worse this time. Whatever it is, we all need to be prepared because the Rumors won't hold back until they control everything.

Now, at least, we all have learned that we can resolve some of our problems by talking about them, creating a plan, and working to build a great friendship. Try not to worry about the Rumors. My friends and I will take care of them."

"Yeah, next time I'll try and talk things out before I go around destroying everything, which, again, I am indeed sorry for doing."

"That's great, Creepo! I am happy we were finally able to help you calm down and talk out what was bothering you. I'm sorry for Brutus and I trying to force you to go away without hearing your side first."

"Thanks, Super Drat. I know you were just trying to protect the goblins and their village."

"The rest of the goblins and myself will work to be more aware of how we make others feel before just kicking them out of the village."

"I like hearing you say that Fred! Sounds like you guys have a great plan ready for action."

"Sure do, and it's all thanks to you and your friends, Super Drat. Now come with me and let's go party with the other goblins, and we can start building our new village tomorrow!"

"Lead the way Fred! Come on Creepo and join the party! It makes me so happy we were able to help and work all of this out for everyone."

10

TIME TO HEAD HOME

"Well, Fred and Creepo, it seems like our work here is done. Another successful mission for now, but with the Rumors out there, I know that can only mean more trouble. But I think it's time for my friends and me to get back home. I have school tomorrow."

"Thanks for helping us, Super Drat, and here—these are for you."

"Wow, thanks, Creepo. These look remarkable."

"Fred and I were able to make these shoes to go with your costume while you were enjoying the party. Not only will they help protect your feet when you're running, but they will also make you run as fast as a charging minotaur."

"Incredible! Thank you so much! These are the coolest shoes ever, and they slip on, so I don't even have to tie them. The goblins make the most incredible gadgets ever. Plus, now that they have Creepo helping them, they will be able to create even more amazing things to use."

Being determined to help Creepo and the goblins worked out pretty well. Making the responsible choice to talk with Creepo sure did make things go a lot smoother.

"Thanks for all your help, Intal. Without your help to think through why Creepo was so upset, we wouldn't have been able to calm him down enough to find out why he was so angry. Thanks again. You'd better get back to your family now."

Tenshi is ready to take us home. Did you say all your goodbyes? Alright, let's head home.

You know, I think I figured out one of your superpowers. You are a great thinker and show a lot of determination. You never give up. That is an extraordinary ability for any superhero to have.

You stuck with me throughout that entire mission. That was remarkable. You certainly helped me out, making good decisions and thinking things through before just jumping into action. All superheroes make mistakes sometimes, but it's important that we learn from those mistakes. When we do, that's how we become stronger.

There is still a lot more to learn about yourself, but at least you got a great start, and there will be plenty more missions for us to do.

Don't feel like you're alone in learning about yourself, because I still have a lot more to learn about myself too. Being a superhero can be tough, but the more you know about yourself and the more comfortable you become with who you are, the more powerful of a superhero you will become in helping to make the world a better place.

I know it can be hard to know exactly who you are. It might even be confusing or frustrating. Before I became Super Drat, I struggled to understand why it was so difficult for me to fit in, especially because I communicated my thoughts and feelings differently. I spent so much time trying to be what everyone else wanted me to be that I never thought about who I was.

Like I said before, I know everyone cares about me, and I love them for that. My parents, my teachers, and my friends all want what is best for me, but sometimes I just need the chance to be me, just like you need a chance to be you.

When we go on our missions, I promise that you can be you, as long as I can be me. I will listen to you and show you respect because as fellow superheroes we need to stick together. And now that we're friends, we can help each other learn even more about who we are and work together as a team. We might even figure out more about your superpowers.

It looks like we finally made it back. I have some homework I need to get done before I go to bed. It shouldn't take me too long.

Remember that being a superhero requires you to be the best hero you can be and the best of your secret identity as well. Homework helps keep my mind in shape. It gets me to think. It's like exercise for my brain, even when it's confusing or frustrating.

Sometimes the homework is too easy, but when it's tough, I treat it like one of my missions. I don't give up until I'm successful, because I stay determined, responsible, assertive, and thoughtful, just like you did on your first mission. And remember that asking for help never hurt any of the great superheroes, and I'm sure it won't ever hurt you.

Chapter 11

DEBRIEF

I am certainly happy that you came with me on this mission. You truly helped me. Even when I thought things were impossible, you stayed with me. I know I have the dragons to help me, and they are awesome, but sometimes it's nice to have a human friend.

Sometimes a friend helps you to think about a task differently. Friends might not always think the same way as you do, but that's what makes them so great. Good friends are hard to come by, but when you find one, it's like finding another superpower.

We were lucky back there with Creepo. Sometimes bullies don't want to talk out their problems. Sometimes they are just too angry or hurt or not even sure about why they act the way they do. It can be hard to just ignore them. That is why it is critical to know when to be assertive and when to ask for help.

Adults are always there to help, but sometimes it is just as essential to have your friends stand by your side. See, the goblins didn't know that what they did made Creepo so upset, and Creepo didn't think anyone cared to hear what he had to say. So instead of talking about the problem, Creepo got angry and did what he did best—he used his superstrength and destroyed stuff.

Sometimes being superstrong doesn't solve the problem. Sometimes solving a problem requires more thought to figure out what the real problem is before you can find the right solution.

Creepo and Fred were two different creatures. Creepo was a supertall, incredibly strong minotaur who could crush things with his hooves and plow things down by charging at them with his long, sharp horns. Fred was a short, intelligent goblin capable of using scraps of garbage to create superamazing gadgets that allowed him to do extraordinary things, like swing from trees using ropes that shot out from bracelets he wore on his wrist.

Even though they were different, in the end they were able to work together and help each other to create something powerful, like my shoes. That is why I always have to remind people that I am not broken. I don't need to be fixed. I am just special. As a superhero, I have met a lot of people and creatures and learned something particularly significant. If we treat people differently because they're different, then we aren't being fair. We should treat everybody the same because we are all the same in that we are all different.

Missions like these make me happy to be a superhero.

Oh no! My dragon senses are going off. Looks like I am needed somewhere else in the world. Keep working on being the best superhero you can be, and maybe we can join forces again. Until next time, may the superhero within you stay strong!

9 781532 075704